DUNK UNDER PRESSURE

Also by Rich Wallace

Winning Season Series

WINNING SEASON

DUNK UNDER PRESSURE

RICH WALLACE

VIKING

VIKING

Published by Penguin Group

Penguin Young Readers Group, 345 Hudson Street, New York, New York 10014, U.S.A.

Penguin Group (Canada), 90 Eglinton Avenue East, Suite 700, Toronto, Ontario, Canada M4P 2Y3
(a division of Pearson Penguin Canada Inc.)

Penguin Books Ltd, 80 Strand, London WC2R 0RL, England

Penguin Ireland, 25 St Stephen's Green, Dublin 2, Ireland (a division of Penguin Books Ltd)

Penguin Group (Australia), 250 Camberwell Road, Camberwell, Victoria 3124, Australia
(a division of Pearson Australia Group Pty Ltd)

Penguin Books India Pvt Ltd, 11 Community Centre, Panchsheel Park, New Delhi - 110 017, India

Penguin Group (NZ), Cnr Airborne and Rosedale Roads, Albany, Auckland 1310, New Zealand
(a division of Pearson New Zealand Ltd)

Penguin Books (South Africa) (Pty) Ltd, 24 Sturdee Avenue, Rosebank, Johannesburg 2196, South Africa

Penguin Books Ltd, Registered Offices: 80 Strand, London WC2R 0RL, England

First published in 2006 by Viking, a division of Penguin Young Readers Group

3 5 7 9 10 8 6 4 2

LIBRARY OF CONGRESS CATALOGING-IN-PUBLICATION DATA
Wallace, Rich.
Dunk under pressure / Rich Wallace.
p. cm. — (Winning season ; #7)
Summary: Free throw specialist Cornell "Dunk" Duncan joins the YMCA summer
basketball league all-star team, but after losing his confidence in an important game
the seventh-grader makes some decisions about becoming an all-around player.
ISBN 0-670-06095-X (hardcover)
[1. Basketball—Fiction. 2. Self-confidence—Fiction. 3. Aunts—Fiction.] I. Title.
PZ7.W15877Dun 2006
[Fic]—dc22
2005023554

Printed in U.S.A.   Set in Caslon 224 Book

FOR JEREMY

• CONTENTS •

1
The Specialist

Cornell Duncan. The guys call him Dunk, but he couldn't dunk from a six-foot ladder. He's flat-footed and slow and jumps about two inches. But he knows the game and is a good defender.

And, man, can he shoot.

Free throws, that is. Put him at the foul line and he doesn't miss.

He made thirty-two in a row one time in practice. Twenty straight is routine.

He makes it look easy.

It isn't.

He'll tell you. Last winter he got cut from the sixth-grade team. Didn't come close to making it. Walked out of the gym blinking back tears and didn't look at a basketball for nearly a week.

Then he read about a college player at Georgetown who led the nation in free-throw percentage. "Easiest shot in the game," the guy said. "Or at least it should be. No one guarding you. Just up, over, and in."

Dunk thought about that and decided that the college player was right. He could shoot free throws. He could make some of them. With a little practice (or a lot), Dunk could become a free-throw magician.

He found a video at the library that demonstrated the perfect technique. Watched it seven times. Then he went to work at it.

He started with a hundred in his narrow driveway every afternoon for a few weeks. When the weather turned icy, he started finding off-moments at the Hudson City YMCA—early in the morning before school, for example, or during the fifteen-minute interval between the evening aerobics classes that his aunt taught.

He could take about sixty shots in those fifteen minutes if his aunt rebounded for him. If she was busy talking to a student, then he'd only shoot thirty. When the second class ended, he'd shoot at least eighty more.

A hundred or more shots a day all winter and spring and into the summer is nearly 25,000 free throws. You shoot that many, you have to get good.

Dunk got real good. So good that he led the YMCA Summer League in free-throw percentage, hitting thirty-five of forty-two shots during the eight-game season. That's eighty-three percent.

Still, he was surprised when he got a call the day after the season ended, inviting him to try out for the league's all-star team. That team would be spending several days at the Shore, competing in the New Jersey YMCA state tournament.

Of course, Dunk still was slow and flat-footed and could barely jump over a worm on the sidewalk. But he definitely caught the coaches' eyes at the tryouts when he hit twenty-three out of twenty-five free throws during warm-ups.

"That kid can shoot," one coach said to another.

"Nice stroke," said the other. "Consistent. He makes the same motion every time. That's the key."

Guys like Spencer Lewis and Jared Owen and Jason Fiorelli—the stars of the middle school's championship team—stopped what they were doing to marvel at Dunk's ability as he worked on his next set of twenty-five. They tried razzing him with whoops and burps and stamping their feet, but Dunk kept his eyes focused on the rim and kept swishing the shots.

"He's like a robot or something," said Fiorelli.

Dunk smiled and sank another one. "Robots got nothing on me," he said, never looking away from the basket.

Still, shooting free throws is only part of the game, so Dunk was not a lock to make the all-star team. His weaknesses were obvious— stronger guys out-muscled him for rebounds, quicker guys darted past him for layups, and springier guys lofted their jump shots over his outstretched arms for buckets.

He had his good moments, too. A rebound and a put-back with Jared all over him; a sweet pass to Miguel Rivera on a give-and-go; a fade-away jumper from fifteen feet (well, maybe it wasn't quite a *jumper*, but a decent shot any-way).

So the coaches figured they might as well keep him. He wouldn't play much, but in the right situation he'd definitely be an asset. They'd seen many close games decided by which team could shoot better from the line.

"Say we're protecting a lead in the final minute and the opposition has to foul somebody to get the ball back," Assistant Coach Red Creighton said in making his case. "You get the ball to Dunk and let 'em foul him. That's two points guaranteed."

"I could see it," said Head Coach Larry Temple, rubbing his jaw. "A free-throw specialist."

So that's why Dunk found his name on the all-star roster after three days of tryouts. He'd made more than eighty-five percent of his free throws over those three days. The best pro and college players only make a little more than ninety percent. Of course that's in the heat of a game, with the heart pounding and the crowd screaming and the intense pressure of competition. Even so, eighty-five percent in practice isn't bad, either. Especially for a kid who's not yet thirteen.

So Dunk was on the twelve-man squad, mostly a practice player, a body to give the first-stringers some competition during workouts. He might get a few minutes of game-time at the tail end of a blowout.

And in the right situation, at the end of a tight game, he just might surprise a few people.

2

Sweaty as a Pig

"Didn't you already practice today?" Aunt Krystal asked a few nights later as Dunk walked onto the YMCA gym floor, dribbling a basketball. "Twice?"

Dunk grinned. With his index finger he straightened his glasses, which had slid down his nose. "The tournament starts tomorrow," he said. "Gotta be sharp." He set the basketball down at the free-throw line and helped his aunt stack some gym mats on the side of the court.

Krystal was dressed in blue running shorts

and a white tank top, and she was sweating from leading the aerobics classes. She was only eight years older than her nephew and was a junior at St. Peter's College in Jersey City. She seemed more like an older sister to Dunk than an aunt.

"Oh yeah, the big-time trip to the Shore," she said. "You guys better win a couple of games; I'm driving down for the semifinals if you get that far."

Dunk shrugged. "The coaches say there'll be some outrageously good teams there. I don't know how we'll stack up."

"You'll do great if you play hard."

"A lot of those teams have been playing together all summer. We've only been a team for a few days. We might get toasted."

"Don't worry about it," Krystal said. "You don't need that kind of pressure at least until high school. You guys are young; you're still little."

Dunk raised his eyebrows and gave his aunt

an amused stare, arching his neck so he was looking down at her. At five-foot-nine, he was three inches taller than she was.

"You know what I mean," she said. "Just have fun."

Krystal knew what she was talking about. She'd been a star athlete in high school, excelling in basketball and track, but had turned down athletic scholarships from Seton Hall and Rutgers. She was well aware of the line between enjoying a sport and making it a job.

"Let me ask you something, Cornell," she said. "How many hours have you spent on basketball today?"

Dunk shrugged. "Three or four," he said.

Krystal raised her eyebrows. "Oh, yeah?"

"Okay, maybe seven." He'd had a team practice session from ten A.M. until noon, then played pickup games on the Y's outside court for most of the afternoon with Spencer and Miguel and a rotating crowd of others. He'd gone through two quarts of water and a bottle of Gatorade playing under that bright, hot sun.

"Do anything else?" Krystal asked.

"Ate a couple of hot dogs," he said with a grin.

"What do you think would happen if you spent maybe *one* of those hours doing something else that you like?"

"I'd be bored?"

"If seven hours of basketball doesn't get boring, then I don't know what else would," Krystal said. "Tell you what you *could* do. Take one of my classes sometime."

"You're kidding, right? Bounce around the gym with a bunch of ladies? To *music*, no less? I don't think so."

The thing was, Dunk couldn't think of anything else he'd rather be doing. As his basketball skills were slowly improving, so was his devotion to the game. Making that all-star team had given his confidence a big boost. He was sure he'd make the school team this winter, but he'd be taking advantage of every opportunity to get better, just in case.

"You're hopeless," Krystal said sweetly, putting her arm around his shoulder and squeezing. "Maybe we could go to the library one of these days. Maybe you can get something to read."

"About basketball?"

"About anything you want."

"Sure," Dunk said. "Maybe there's a book about rebounding."

Krystal shook her head slowly. "All you ate today was some hot dogs?"

"Yeah. It was too hot to eat much."

"You hungry now?"

"Very."

"Come on. Let's get something. I'm buying."

"Can you wait ten minutes?"

"I suppose so," Krystal said, putting on a light sweatshirt. "Why?"

Dunk picked up the basketball and started

dribbling. "Fifty free throws," he said. "If you rebound for me, it'll go faster."

"Looks like it rained," Krystal said as they stepped out of the YMCA. The setting sun was shining, but some dark clouds were moving rapidly away toward New York City. The Boulevard was steaming.

"For about eight seconds," Dunk said. "I've never seen such a quick shower. It sure didn't cool things off."

"So what do you feel like eating?" Krystal asked. "And don't say another hot dog."

"Pizza?"

"I had it last night. Chinese, maybe? I'm thinking Hunan vegetables and a shrimp roll."

"Sounds good."

Hudson City's main street was lined with small shops and restaurants of all types: Mexican, Cuban, Thai, Italian, and many others. The languages and skin tones of the city's residents were as varied as could be. So was the music that poured out of the shops.

The nearby choices for Chinese food were the Jade Palace, with its carpeted dining room and booths and waitresses, or the tiny Beijing Kitchen across the street, which relied mostly on take-out orders but had a handful of stools at the counter.

They stopped on the sidewalk outside the Jade Palace and Krystal gave Dunk a good looking-over. "You're sweaty as a pig," she said. "And the food's better over there anyway."

"You're a little damp yourself," Dunk said. "Or is that an indelicate thing to say?"

"*Pffft,*" Krystal replied. "Where'd you find a word like *indelicate*? There's nothing wrong with a bit of honest perspiration."

So they crossed the street and sat at the stools in front of the Beijing Kitchen's open kitchen, where they could watch the food being prepared.

The skinny young guy behind the counter nodded at Krystal and started to flirt. He obviously recognized her. "This your big brother?" he asked.

"My *little* nephew."

"Oh, sorry," the guy said. He looked mischievously at Dunk. "I better bring you the children's menu."

Dunk laughed. "Only if I can get three dinners off it."

The phone rang and the guy answered, writing down an order. Behind him, two men were working frantically over giant woks, clattering and stirring, and a woman was assembling orders: putting rice into white cardboard containers, ladling soup into plastic bowls, tossing packets of mustard and soy sauce into bags.

"You decide yet?" the guy asked after hanging up the phone.

"What's good tonight?" Krystal asked.

"Everything's good, beautiful." He winked.

Krystal rolled her eyes but didn't seem to mind the compliment. She ordered the Hunan vegetables.

Dunk asked for shrimp with snow peas.

"You guys want soup?"

"I don't know," Dunk said. "It's so hot out."

"Nice and cool in here," the guy said, pointing to a small window air conditioner that seemed to be laboring hard. The restaurant wasn't very cool at all.

"Okay. Wonton for me," Dunk said. "A small one."

"Only one size," the guy said. "Half a pint."

"Half a pint? That's almost a whole pint!"

The guy looked at Dunk like he was crazy. But Dunk thought the joke was hilarious.

"Egg drop," said Krystal. "And don't mind my nephew. His sense of humor is a little off."

"Chopsticks for the dinners?"

"Of course," said Krystal.

"Not for me," Dunk said. "Bring me a fork and a spoon. I'm starving."

There was a rumble of thunder after dinner as they walked toward Fourth Street, down on the residential end of the Boulevard. Dunk lived two blocks to the left, toward the Hudson River, and Krystal was a block to the right. In the past there would have been no question that she would escort him to his door. But suddenly it occurred to Dunk that it was time for a shift.

So he turned right on Fourth Street.

"You're walking *me* home?" Krystal said with an amused grin. "I don't think so."

"Why not?" Dunk said. "I know my way around."

"True," she said hesitantly, stopping in her tracks.

"It's barely even dark yet."

She put her hand on her chin, weighing her options. Dunk was big for his age. And it was

only three blocks from her apartment to his house.

"Okay," she said, "but you go straight home. And call me right away."

"I will."

"Don't even bother. I'll call your mom as soon as I get in and stay on the line until you get there."

Dunk laughed. "It's quarter after nine. I don't usually get in until almost ten in the summer."

"Well, when you're with me you do. I don't care how tall you get, you're still a little squirt to me."

"Don't worry, I'm going straight home. I gotta get up early tomorrow, remember?" He patted himself on the chest. "All-star basketball player. The bus for the Shore leaves at eight."

Dunk waited for his aunt to get in, then walked quickly home. The streets weren't very busy, at least not this far downtown. He crossed the Boulevard and headed up toward Jefferson

Elementary School, which was only about fifty yards from his house. When he'd been a student there, he would wait till the absolute last minute to leave for school, watching from the kitchen window until all the other kids were lined up and about to enter the building.

He'd never been late, but he'd come close a few times. His third-grade teacher used to call him "Last-Second Duncan." But Dunk didn't care.

His mom and dad were sitting on the couch in the small living room, watching the news on TV.

"Here he is," Mom was saying into the phone. She gave Dunk a smile.

"Good night, Aunt Krystal," Dunk said loudly.

Dad tossed a pillow in Dunk's direction, and he snatched it from the air.

"Quick reflexes," Dad said.

"Gotta have 'em."

"You packed yet?"

"Nah. It'll take me about nine seconds. It's only two nights. At least it better be."

It was a single-elimination tournament, so an early loss would cut the trip short. But Dunk and his teammates were confident.

"There's an article in the paper about you guys," Dad said, pointing toward the *Hudson Dispatch* that was lying on the coffee table.

"Oh, yeah?" Dunk picked up the paper and found the sports section.

"Toward the back," Dad said.

Dunk found the three-paragraph article under the heading Local Briefs.

Hudson City Youth Team
Bound for State Tourney
TOMS RIVER—Sixteen basketball squads from throughout New Jersey will vie for the state YMCA eleven-to-twelve-year-old title Tuesday through Thursday at the Greater Monmouth YMCA. Among the entries is an all-star team comprised of players from

the Hudson City YMCA summer
league.

Veteran Coach Larry Temple leads
the local team, which includes several
members of the Hudson City Middle
School squad that won the East Jersey
Conference title last winter. Center
Jared Owen and forward Jason Fiorelli
are two of HC's standouts.

Camden is the tournament's two-
time defending champion. This will be
the Hudson City Y's first appearance in
the event.

"Not much of a write-up," Dunk said. "Hope
they'll give us some better press when we win
the thing."

"*If* you win it," Mom said. "Don't get arrogant
now."

"Don't worry."

"Krystal says you ate?"

"Yeah, but I'm still hungry."

"Eat some fruit," Mom said. "Listen, Cornell, we got you some stuff for the trip." She opened a plastic shopping bag and took out a bottle of sunscreen, a toothbrush and a small tube of toothpaste, and a box of Band-aids. Then she held up a pair of red shoelaces. "Your team color," she said.

Dunk laughed. "I think the guys will bust my chops if I show up in red laces. Where'd you get all this stuff anyway?"

"Down at Amazing Ray's."

Ray's was a discount store on the Boulevard that had everything under the sun.

"Well, thanks," Dunk said. "Wish you guys could come see the games." He held up the laces. "I'll keep these as a spare, for good luck. We can always use some of that."

3
Nervous Tension

*T*he Hudson City school bus pulled into a parking spot outside the Greater Monmouth YMCA after a two-hour trip down the Garden State Parkway.

"I don't see no beach," Jason Fiorelli said loudly.

"We're four miles inland," Coach Temple said in his raspy voice, standing and facing the players as the bus pulled to a stop. He was a monstrous man, with the height of a former power forward but the weight of one who'd spent the past forty years working behind the desk at his accounting office. "Don't worry—we'll be staying in a hotel right near the Boardwalk. *If* we win this game, that is. Otherwise it's 'Sayonara, Shore.'"

Sixteen YMCAs had sent teams to the three-day tournament, but half of those teams would be going home early. There'd be eight games today, with the winners advancing to tomorrow's round and earning a night at the Shore. Four games tomorrow would cut the field down for that evening's semifinals. The championship game was the next afternoon.

Dunk followed his teammates off the bus. They stood in the parking lot for a few moments, looking at the city names on the other buses.

"Camden," said Spencer Lewis, who was wearing reflective sunglasses, a loose Hawaiian shirt, and sandals. "That's a big-time basketball town."

"Atlantic City," Dunk said, pointing across

the lot. "Paterson. Burlington. Morristown."

Fiorelli looked toward the sky and sniffed. "You smell that salt air?" he said to Dunk. He sniffed twice more. "I think I do."

"That's Spencer's armpits," Dunk said with a wicked grin. "Nervous tension, you know?"

Spencer gave Dunk's shoulder a light punch. Spencer had always been a combative kid, but he had a brotherly respect for Dunk's odd sense of humor. "I owe you one for that," he said.

"Let's hustle, boys!" called Coach Temple. "We're in the second game."

The brackets were posted on a large bulletin board outside the gym:

TUESDAY

Game I, 10 A.M. West Trenton vs. Morristown

Game 2, 11:15 A.M. Hudson City vs. Salem

Game 3, 12:30 P.M. Camden vs. Passaic

Game 4, 1:45 P.M. Somerset vs. Hackensack

Game 5, 3 P.M. Atlantic City vs. Paterson

Game 6, 4:15 P.M. Montclair vs. Monmouth
Game 7, 5:30 P.M. Elizabeth vs. Gloucester
Game 8, 6:45 P.M. Burlington vs. Newark

WEDNESDAY
Game I winner vs. Game 2 winner, 9 A.M.
Game 3 winner vs. Game 4 winner, 10:15 A.M.
Game 5 winner vs. Game 6 winner, 11:30 A.M.
Game 7 winner vs. Game 8 winner, 12:45 P.M.
Semifinals: 6 P.M. and 7:15 P.M.

THURSDAY
Consolation game (semifinal losers), 10:45 A.M.
Championship game, noon

Dunk followed the others into the gym and looked around. This was a big place—like a college gym—with bleachers on both sides of a shiny hardwood floor. There were large scoreboards on both sides of the court.

The squads from West Trenton and Morristown were warming up at opposite baskets. They looked smooth and confident. The bleachers were about half full, mostly with players and coaches from the other teams.

And now Dunk could feel his own armpits starting to drip with nervous sweat. It wouldn't be long before they'd be on that court, facing a win-or-go-home opening game. Nobody on this team wanted to take a bus ride back so quickly. The excitement of a potential state title had them feeling wired.

"Downstairs," Coach Temple said firmly, pointing toward a sign that said LOCKERS. "Team meeting first, then we'll suit up and relax for a few minutes."

Dunk wasn't even sure why he was nervous. He didn't expect to play much, if at all. The pressure would be on guys like Fiorelli and Jared and Spencer.

He looked over at Jason Fiorelli—the guy who always seemed to make the clutch shot or get the steal when the game was on the line. But Fiorelli was lacking his usual confident expression.

"You all right?" Dunk asked as they made their way down the stairs.

Fiorelli shrugged, then smiled. "It's weird, with these teams from all over the state," he said. "When you're playing Jersey City or Bayonne, you know what you're up against, right? But I don't even know where Salem is. I never heard of some of the towns on that list."

"You ain't been around much, have you?" said Spencer, turning to look back at them. He was grinning. These guys loved to ride each other.

"More than you have," Fiorelli said.

"You never heard of Camden?"

"Camden I heard of. Camden is the man."

"You think New Jersey is, like, this big," Spencer said, holding his thumbs and forefingers together to make a small circle. "Hudson City, Jersey City, Weehawken, Newark. That's hardly any of it."

"No kidding?" Fiorelli said sarcastically. "You mean there's more to the world than what I see out my window? Thanks, Mr. Geography. Tell me more."

They reached the locker room and took seats on the benches. Coach told them that they'd keep the plays basic since they'd only had three practice sessions since the tryouts. He hoped he'd get everyone some playing time, but that would depend on how close the games were.

"We're here to win," he said. "I don't know if you guys realize what a great basketball state this is. Some of the people in this tournament will go on to be big-time college players. Maybe even pros."

"We got one right here, Coach," said Fiorelli, pointing at Spencer. "Spencer Lewis, professional geographer."

"That's nice, Jason," Coach said. "Now how about getting serious?"

"No problem, Coach. Just breaking the tension a little."

Coach said that Willie Shaw and Spencer would start at guard, with Jared at center and Fiorelli and Ryan Grimes at forward. That was the same lineup that had won the middle-school league championship the previous winter. They'd been split up on different teams for the summer league, but they obviously knew one another well.

Jared was the big scorer, a tall, strong kid who grabbed a ton of rebounds and rarely missed a layup. Spencer, the vocal point guard, was the leader on the floor, bringing the ball up and controlling the offense. Fiorelli was all about speed and enthusiasm. Ryan and Willie were fierce defenders who knew their roles and helped the machine keep rolling.

Dunk put up his hand.

"Yeah?" Coach said.

"Where the heck is Salem anyway?"

"They're probably out in the bleachers."

"No, I mean, where *is* it? We never even heard of it."

Coach laughed. "Way south," he said. "Down by Delaware. As far from Hudson City as you can get and still be in New Jersey."

"Let's send 'em back in a hurry," Spencer said, pulling his red-and-black jersey over his head. "Show them what Hudson City basketball is about."

West Trenton finished off a tight win over Morristown, and the Hudson City players took the court. They were used to smaller gyms with less light and older floors, so this place would take some getting used to.

"It's almost too much space," Fiorelli said during warm-ups after missing a couple of shots from beyond the three-point arc. "The walls are so far away, it throws off your focus."

"The baskets are still ten feet high," Dunk said.

"Yeah. But it just feels different."

Dunk stepped to the free-throw line. Fiorelli was right—things did look different with all that space behind the baseline. So he talked himself through the motion—crouch slightly with the ball in your fingertips, rise with some force and use that leg strength to help propel the ball. Flick the wrist of the shooting hand. Keep the arc high and soft—never a line drive.

He took four shots and made three of them. And then he took his seat on the bench.

The Hudson City Hornets seemed out of sync in the opening minutes, and Salem's deliberate style—get the ball inside to the taller players— paid off with an early 7–2 lead.

"They're patient and they look for good shots," Coach Temple said during a timeout. "We need to shake them up a little, apply some pressure."

"And we need to run," Spencer said. "That's our game. Fast breaks, layups, energy. We're too flat out there."

Fiorelli finally connected on a jumper after two bad misses, then Jared ripped down a defensive rebound to start a fast break that ended with Willie's layup. The game quickly shifted to Hudson City's run-and-gun style, and the Hornets gradually built a lead. Coach started working substitutes into the game, too. But Dunk stayed on the bench.

The starters took the floor again for the second half, and Fiorelli's hot shooting and Jared's dominance inside put the game out of reach by the middle of the fourth quarter.

"Dunk, go in for Jared," Coach said while the action stopped for a free throw. "Get us some rebounds."

Dunk reported in and jogged toward the end of the court, tapping Jared on the shoulder and taking his place as a Salem forward prepared to shoot. Dunk glanced at the scoreboard; Hudson City had a 46–31 advantage with just under four minutes to play.

The Salem player next to him was several

inches taller and very lean. He was their center—their best offensive threat—and had played
every minute of the game.

Box out, Dunk thought, reminding himself to
get his body between that opponent and the basket, planting himself firmly to get in a good position for the rebound.

But the free throw hit the front of the rim
and bounced over Dunk's outstretched hands.
The Salem center grabbed the ball, leaned into
Dunk, then quickly pivoted and drove toward
the basket, making an easy layup.

"Bad bounce," Fiorelli said as Dunk ran past
him. "Wake up, now. They're pressing!"

Salem's defenders were all over the Hudson
City players, feverishly trying to get the ball
back. But Spencer took Willie's inbounds pass
and calmly dribbled up the court, shielding the
ball from the guard who was hounding him all
the way.

Dunk ran toward the basket and set up just

outside the paint. He could feel the Salem center's hand pressing firmly between his shoulder blades and see his extra-large sneakers on either side of Dunk's feet. The guy wasn't giving an inch.

And suddenly the ball was screaming toward Dunk, a wickedly quick bounce pass courtesy of Spencer. Dunk gripped the leather with both hands and looked for an open man. Fiorelli was waving from the corner, but Dunk could see the gold-and-blue uniform of a defender in close pursuit.

The Salem center was all over Dunk, but the smart play was to drive to the basket. He dribbled once with his back toward the goal, then tipped his left shoulder into his opponent and shot with his right hand.

Wham. The ball was violently swatted away, but instantly the referee's whistle blew. Dunk had been fouled. His forearm stung from the blow.

"Shake it off," Spencer said. "Hit these."

Dunk nodded toward Spencer. That little bit of action had pumped him up, shaking the nervousness from his system. The horn blew, and two more Hudson City subs—David Choi and Lamont Wilkins—ran onto the court, replacing Spencer and Fiorelli.

Dunk bounced the ball with both hands and let out his breath. He ran through the motion in his head, smooth and consistent, eyes above the rim. And then he calmly sank the shot. The second one rippled through the net as well, and Dunk was in the books with a pair of free throws.

That was all the scoring for him, but he managed a rebound and an assist and felt great about his contribution. Hudson City had moved comfortably into the second round. They'd be spending the night at the Shore.

"Good work," Fiorelli said, punching Dunk on the arm.

"Yow," Dunk said in alarm.

"I barely touched you."

"Yeah, but that's where I got smacked." He examined his forearm, where a bruise was forming. "No big deal. I'll survive."

"A battle wound," Fiorelli said. "You earned it."

"Thanks. That's probably all for me, though. You'd have to build another big lead like that before I'd play again."

"Yeah. Trenton looked really good in that first game. We'll have to play our butts off to beat them tomorrow."

"Right," Dunk said. "And look at these guys." He pointed to the Camden players warming up for the next game. "We'll have to get by them just to make the final."

"They've won this tournament two times in a row," Fiorelli said.

"Two times?" Dunk said. "That's almost three times!"

Fiorelli gave Dunk the same confused look the guy at the Beijing Kitchen had. Then he shook his head and smiled. "I'll worry about basketball tomorrow. Let's get to the beach. Enjoy this trip while we can."

4
Mind Games

The Holiday Inn was about five hundred yards from the beach and the Boardwalk, and the marquee outside the hotel read WELCOME BASKETBALL ALL-STARS.

"Does that mean us?" Fiorelli exclaimed as the bus pulled in. He was eating a box of raisins.

"All eight teams are staying here," Coach Temple said. "We'll be bumping elbows with the whole tournament brigade."

"Cool," said Spencer. "We'll make sure nobody sleeps."

Coach gave Spencer a friendly glare. "Better make sure *you* all sleep," he said. "We've got two hard games tomorrow, assuming we win the first one."

"No problem," Spencer replied. "We'll rest on the beach this afternoon. Most of the teams won't even get here till later."

Coach read off the room assignments: three players to a room, with two beds and a cot. "Split it up any way you want, but I think the starters ought to have a bed, not a cot," he said. "But you can draw straws or cut cards to work it out if you want. No fistfights."

Everybody laughed at that. Dunk was assigned a room with David and Willie. Dunk set his backpack on the cot, but Willie said he could have the bed.

"You'd be hanging off that thing, Dunk."

"Thanks, bro."

Even though Willie was a starter, he gladly took the cot. He was only five-foot-one, wiry, and very competitive. The cot was plenty big for him.

Dunk brushed his teeth, then they changed into swimming shorts, grabbed their sunglasses, and met everyone else in the lobby.

"Pool or ocean?" Jared asked, sporting leather sandals and a Yankees cap.

"The ocean, without question," said Spencer. "Save the pool for tonight. Let's catch some waves."

"Wait a minute," said Fiorelli, who was wearing long blue-and-white surfer shorts and a T-shirt that said GYM RAT. "We gotta eat first."

"At the beach!" Spencer said. "You can get anything you want on the Boardwalk—sausage sandwiches, french fries, corn on the cob. It's like a mile-long carnival out there."

"Then let's get there."

"I ain't stopping you."

Dunk looked around at the group of players as they walked toward the beach. He'd never really been part of the crowd before, never had what could be called a best friend. He was friendly with lots of kids, but most afternoons and weekends he went his own way.

He was most content to hang out with his family. His dad worked for the Hudson City Department of Public Works—fixing roads, plowing snow in the winter, doing landscaping in the small city parks. He and Dunk played chess together or watched TV in the evenings.

Dunk's mom worked as a nurse at a hospital in Jersey City. Her best friend was her younger sister, Dunk's aunt Krystal. The four of them were as close as can be.

But this summer Dunk had begun to branch out, playing games of pickup basketball at the Y and sometimes stopping off for tacos or a soda with guys like Willie and Lamont.

So when they reached the beach he felt comfortable spreading out his towel on the hot sand with the others, and he knew it was all in fun when Spencer tackled him at the edge of the surf and gave him a too-quick immersion in the cool water. Later he was glad to share his giant sleeve of fries with whoever wanted some, and to trade insults back and forth about their hair (Dunk's was shaved close to his head) or their physiques (only Spencer, Lamont, and Miguel had any muscle to speak of; the rest were either too lean like Fiorelli and Willie or on the pudgy side like Louie and Dunk).

Around four thirty, Spencer decided that they should head back to the hotel. "Before these white guys burn to a crisp," he said to Dunk, pointing toward Fiorelli and Jared.

"No problem here," Fiorelli said. "My mom made me pack thirty-SPF sunblock lotion. Nothing gets through that."

Dunk looked at his own dark arms. He'd put on lotion, too, but he must have been sloppy about it. His shoulders felt hot and slightly sore.

"You missed your nose," Dunk said to

Fiorelli. "It's as red as a strawberry."

Fiorelli quickly put his hand to his face. "Get out!" he said. "Is it really?"

"It's glowing!" Spencer said, delighted. "That thirty-SPF ain't worth a thing if you forget to put it on!"

"I put it on," Fiorelli said. He felt his nose again. "Ouch. I guess I *did* miss that part."

"Well," Dunk said, "at least you won't get lost if you walk on the beach tonight. That nose will be shining like Rudolph's."

After dinner they hung around the pool and tossed a Frisbee in the hotel parking lot. The place was crawling with kids their age from all over the state. The coaches did their best to keep things quiet, but they were outnumbered by the basketball players.

The cool water felt good on Dunk's shoulders as he leaned against the side of the pool, watching Spencer and Willie and some kids from

Camden do cannonballs off the diving board. Only Dunk's head was above the water.

"Who you play for?" asked a kid who was swimming up to Dunk. He stood and shook water from his head. He had to be at least six feet tall.

"Hudson City."

"You guys any good?"

"We're here, aren't we?"

"You're here. But who'd you beat to get here?"

"Salem."

The guy smirked. His hair was razor-cut short but he was wearing a yellow sweatband around his head. He grabbed the edge of the pool and hauled himself up, taking a seat above Dunk. "They're kind of weak, aren't they?"

"They were okay. We handled 'em."

"You a starter?"

"Nah," Dunk said. "Who you with?"

"Your next opponent." The kid grinned broadly. "We saw your game."

"Then why'd you ask me how we did?"

The kid shrugged. "Just testing you, I suppose."

Dunk ran his hand along the surface of the water, skimming it and creating a small wave. "We started slow today, but then we hammered 'em. And Coach gave the subs a lot of playing time."

"So maybe it was your subs I saw. I missed the first half—team meeting and all. But that couldn't have been your best players out there at the beginning of the second half. Must have been the scrubs . . . I mean subs."

Dunk didn't comment. He could tell that this guy was trying to psyche him out, and that he hoped Dunk would relay that feeling of insecurity to his teammates. But Dunk wasn't biting. He wouldn't be fooled by that kind of talk.

"I guess you'll find out tomorrow," Dunk said, swimming a few strokes away. "Hope you don't have nightmares. Those Salem guys probably will."

The kid laughed. "Your nightmare starts tomorrow morning. As soon as we take the court."

The Hudson City coaches ordered all of the players to their rooms at ten P.M., with lights out by eleven. Dunk had to step over David's gym bag and video-game player and Willie's sneakers and two empty soda cans and his own backpack to get into bed, where he spread out on the sheets and propped his head up on two fat pillows. The TV was tuned to a music channel.

Coach Temple knocked on the door. David opened it, and Coach said, "All accounted for? Good. Keep it quiet now and get some sleep."

Ten minutes later there was a softer rap on the door. David groaned. "I got it last time," he said. He balled up a sock and threw it in Dunk's direction. "Your turn."

Dunk rolled out of bed and immediately

stepped on one of the soda cans. "Ouch!" he said. "I can't see."

David turned on a light and threw his other sock at Dunk, who hopped past the debris on the floor and opened the door.

Spencer was standing there, looking mischievous. He slipped into the room, followed by Miguel and Fiorelli.

"You didn't think we'd go to sleep this early on vacation, did you?" Spencer said.

"It's not a vacation," Willie said sharply, sitting up on his cot, wearing just his plain white underwear. "This is the state tournament, man."

"I know it. But how often do we get to take road trips? Lighten up."

"I'm tired," Willie said. "That sun zapped me on the beach. And we've got a tough game first thing in the morning."

"Yeah. Well, maybe I'm too nervous to sleep," Spencer said, sitting on the edge of David's bed. "Besides, half the other teams are still out by the pool. Can't you hear them?"

"We brought food," Miguel said, holding up bags of pretzels and M&Ms.

"You better not get caught in here," Willie said. "The coaches'll bench us all."

"The coaches already checked the rooms," Spencer replied. "They *did* check this one, right?"

"Yeah. But don't get crazy, or they'll come back."

"We won't stay long," Fiorelli said. "And Spencer wasn't kidding. We *are* nervous. Some of those guys on the other teams are big. And *really* athletic."

"They're just as nervous as we are," Dunk said, shoving his backpack closer to his bed with his foot. "One guy from Trenton was busting my chops at the pool, trying to make it seem like we got lucky drawing Salem in the first round. But he knew we were good; I could tell."

"The guy with the yellow headband?" Miguel asked. "He tried the same thing on me. Playing mind games."

The six players talked for half an hour longer. They had varying levels of athletic experience— Dunk had played on only a few real teams, while Spencer, Miguel, Willie, and Fiorelli had been starters on football, basketball, or baseball teams for several years. David had experienced the pressure of pitching for the school team the previous spring. They all knew that when teams were evenly matched talent-wise, the deciding factor was usually psychological.

"The ones that win championships are the ones that don't choke up in a tight situation," Spencer was saying. "You stay focused and do what you do best. Hit the clutch single, make the interception. Or just perform like you always do and wait for the other guy to screw up."

"You got it," Fiorelli said. "Today we started out slow, but we just took care of business and outplayed 'em. There'll be a lot of pressure the rest of this tournament, but we got that mental advantage. We definitely know how to win."

Dunk hadn't thought about it much before, but these guys were right. He'd become a pretty good basketball player over the past few months, and was very good at the one thing he practiced most. The next step was to develop the kind of attitude that Spencer and Fiorelli had.

An attitude that didn't leave room for failure.

5
High Intensity

West Trenton had a talented team, with a pair of quick guards and a couple of big, strong players inside. The score went back and forth throughout the first half, with neither team ever gaining more than a four-point lead.

Any time one team threatened to open up some breathing room, either Fiorelli or one of the Trenton guards seemed to hit a key shot. When Fiorelli fired in an off-balance three-pointer with two seconds left on the clock before halftime, it gave the Hornets a one-point advantage as they headed to the locker rooms.

"You're looking like the MVP of this whole tournament," Dunk said to Fiorelli as they hustled out of the gym.

Jason gave a tight smile. "Thanks," he said, "but there's a long way to go. I don't know how that last shot went in; they had two guys in my face, and I was totally out of breath."

The starters had played nearly every minute, with only two other Hornets getting on the court for brief appearances. West Trenton had stuck with its best players, too. The tall kid with the yellow headband who'd confronted Dunk at the pool had stayed seated. He gave Dunk a friendly wave once during a timeout. Dunk gave him a thumbs-up sign and a smirk.

"Two things," Coach Temple said as the players sprawled on the benches and leaned against lockers. "First, it's pretty obvious that these guys can run with us, so our biggest advantage is neutralized. That doesn't mean we shouldn't keep looking for the fast break, but we've been out of control on a few of them. We can't expect to just outrun them; there's gotta be some good passing as well.

"Second, our shot selection has not been great, even though a lot of them are connecting."

Coach looked directly at Fiorelli, who was on the floor with his back against a locker, his feet sticking straight out and a towel over his head. "Jason, a few of those buckets you made had no business going in. It must be your lucky day. Keep shooting, but let's move the ball around a bit more and set up some better shots. Willie and Ryan are barely touching the ball. You've got to get all five guys involved in the offense."

"Sounds good to me," Fiorelli said. "It's hard to find Willie, though. He's, like, three feet shorter than anybody else out there."

"Look harder," Coach said, obviously amused.

"Maybe we could paint a big white X on Willie's jersey or something," Spencer said. "Or spray his hair yellow."

"Tell you what," Willie said. "We win this tournament, you can spray my hair any color you want. In the meantime, just get me the ball."

The intensity rose even higher in the second half, and the score stayed tight as can be. Spencer made a real effort to pass the ball to Willie, who was a good ball-handler and passer. But the man guarding him was a half-foot taller and had a wide wingspan. The only shot Willie managed to take the entire game was a fast-break layup.

West Trenton's yellow-sweatbanded sub got off the bench to cover Jared for a few minutes, but he was awkward and slow and Jared scored four quick points to give the Hornets a five-point advantage.

Dunk sat through the whole thing, of course, but his stomach was tight and his breathing was intense, just as if he was out there on the court. He knew he wasn't ready to be a big contributor to this team, but he was part of it nonetheless. He felt the sting of every missed shot and the joy of every made one, was just as humbled any time a Trenton guard faked out Spencer or Willie with a quick stutter step, and felt the pounding of bodies as Jared and Ryan battled their opponents for rebounds.

He'd played a lot of basketball against those guys. He knew how tough and determined they were.

This was his passion; this was his sport. He'd keep working on his game, his endurance, his court smarts. He'd get there. He'd be a player.

In the end, Jared's punishing play under the basket was enough to make the difference. Hudson City played a smart, patient game down the stretch, cementing a three-point victory and a spot in that evening's semifinals.

Walking across the court, Dunk felt a hand on his shoulder. It was the tall kid with the sweatband. "I guess you guys *are* pretty good, aren't you?" he said.

"Guess so," Dunk replied. "I can't take any credit, though. All I earned today were some splinters in my butt."

"I got a few myself," the guy said, laughing. "Plus a nice elbow to the throat from your center." He put a hand to his neck and winced. "Good luck the rest of the way. We wanted a shot at Camden tonight. Hope you can knock them off instead."

"That'd be something," Dunk said. "I'll be yelling my head off. Not much else I can do."

"Tonight at seven fifteen," Dunk said into his cell phone.

"I'll be down," said Aunt Krystal. "Your mom

and dad won't get there, though. They'd have to leave work by four to beat the traffic. No way they can do that."

"No problem," Dunk said.

"So you won this morning?"

"Real tight, but yeah. I didn't get in. It went right down to the wire."

"That's the best kind of game," Krystal said.

"Not if you're a sub."

"I guess not."

"No problem," Dunk said. "It was exciting just to watch."

"Should be fun tonight."

"Fun? We're playing against Camden, Krystal. It'll be hard!"

"One hour on the beach, maximum!" Coach Temple said as the players got off the bus outside the hotel. "I don't want you frying in the sun. Some of you might even want to take a *nap* this afternoon instead, gentlemen. Camden's got a deep roster. Their top guys only played half the game this morning."

"I'm very energy-efficient, Coach," Fiorelli said. "I got this metabolism that can go all day. I'm fueled by raisins and sunlight."

"Yeah, well we'll see how energy-efficient you are in the fourth quarter tonight. Believe me, you'll be running nonstop against those guys."

So all of the starters and a few others stayed by the pool after Coach promised they'd get some major beach time the following afternoon after the tournament ended.

Dunk walked to the beach with David, Miguel, and Lamont.

On the surface, David Choi was a quiet, serious kid, but he had a sly sense of humor. He'd spent the entire game this morning on the bench, just like Dunk had. But he was a talented player, and had been a big reason why Lupita Records had won the YMCA summer league title. He and Spencer had been a formidable one-two scoring punch, and Lamont had been a force inside.

Dunk had played for Envigado Bakery, which finished 4–4. Ryan Grimes was the only other player from Envigado to make the all-star team.

"You played an outstanding game this morning, Lamont," David teased, grinning so widely you could see his full set of braces.

Lamont was a strong guy and nobody usually messed with him. But he looked surprised. He'd only been off the bench for a brief segment late in the first half after Jared picked up his second foul.

"Six seconds, wasn't it?" David said.

Lamont looked away with an embarrassed smile. "Had to be sixteen, at least," he said.

Only eight men had played for Hudson City, as Coach left his starters on the floor throughout the close contest.

"Maybe twelve," David said. "A *crucial* twelve seconds, though. Big-time."

"And how many seconds did you get?" Lamont asked. "I think it was something like *zero*."

"Something like that," David conceded. "I lost count."

They reached the beach and Dunk knelt down to take off his sandals. The sand was scorching hot, though, so he quickly put them back on. "We better set up by the water," he said. "It must be a hundred degrees out here."

"Not too far from the food," Miguel said. He inhaled deeply. The fried and grilled foods on the Boardwalk smelled delicious and tempting. "I could go for some eats. Anybody else?"

"Always," Dunk said. "Let's see—I smell hamburgers, cotton candy . . . fried chicken, maybe ice cream. Can you smell ice cream from this far away? Probably not."

"Caramel corn!" Lamont said. "I definitely smell that."

"Tell you what," Dunk said. "Ten minutes in

the water, then we try as many foods as we can stomach. We got all afternoon to digest."

"And all evening, too," David said, "if the game goes the way I think it will. Too bad for you, though, Lamont. Coach said he's planning on using you for another ten seconds. You better watch what you eat."

"You better watch what you say," Lamont replied with a laugh. "Or the next thing you'll be tasting is ocean water."

After a quick swim they made their way up to the Boardwalk, awed by the great variety of rides and miniature golf and games of chance and food stands. There was a place to shoot basketballs to win prizes and a huge merry-go-round and a Ferris wheel.

The boys plunked down quarters on numbers, trying to win CDs and candy bars, then accumulated prize tickets at Skee Ball and target shooting.

"I got twenty-four tickets," Lamont said as they walked across the arcade. "That has to be worth a lot."

"Maybe a Corvette or a trip to Hawaii," David joked.

"Probably a Tootsie Roll," Dunk said. "Let's check it out."

The prize counter was lined with stuffed animals, cheap CD players, T-shirts, and other glitzy stuff. Inside the counter the shelves held whistles and candy and smaller toys.

"You could get a deck of cards if you had sixteen more tickets," David said.

"I already spent three bucks winning these," Lamont replied. He settled for a small plastic comb for twenty tickets. He handed his extra tickets to a little kid who was eyeing a baseball on a shelf.

"I'm the big winner today," Lamont said, running the comb through his hair. "Anybody wants to borrow this thing, it'll cost you a quarter."

"A quarter? That's almost half a dollar," Dunk said, giggling at his own lame joke.

The others just looked at him, shaking their heads.

"Listen, Dunk," said David. He pointed toward the basketball-shooting stand. "You're Mr. Free Throw, right? You ought to be able to win hugely over there."

Dunk studied the setup. The basket was about fifteen feet high, and the rims were very narrow. "Doesn't look fair," he said, "but I guess I could handle it."

The deal was two shots for a dollar. Make them both and you'd win a big stuffed animal. Make one and you got a candy bar.

Dunk paid his dollar and took the ball. He bounced it a couple of times and realized that it was off balance, probably weighted slightly on one side just to make things more difficult. He eyed the rim, then turned to his friends with a wry smile. "This ain't what I'd call sporting," he said.

"Come on," Lamont said. He turned to the teenager who was running the show. "Dunk is the wizard of Hudson City," he said. "He never misses."

"No pressure, Dunk," David said. "Just make believe you're in your driveway."

Dunk went through his normal motion, sending the ball on a graceful arc above the rim. But it hit the back iron and rolled out. The other guys groaned. Dunk laughed.

"Come *on*, Dunk," Miguel said with exaggerated enthusiasm. "We need this, baby. We can split that candy bar four ways. We're starving."

"It's all you," Lamont added. "Gotta have it. This is big."

And Dunk made the shot. He took the chocolate bar and held it above his head with one hand as the others applauded.

"Split that in four," he said, handing the bar to Miguel. He started walking directly toward the nearest refreshment stand. "It's time for some *real* eating now, boys. Everything smells so good."

6

25,000 Shots

*T*onight's game was huge, and they knew it. Camden was known as a basketball town; its two public high school teams were regularly ranked among the best in the state, and their graduates could be found on college rosters in the Big East and the ACC and even in the NBA. And obviously its youth programs were top-notch as well. They'd been the dominant team in this tournament so far.

A sizeable crowd had gathered to watch. About half of the Hudson City players had relatives in the bleachers, but there were many more on hand from Camden. Aunt Krystal was up there in the tenth row. She gave Dunk a wink and made a fist.

Camden had breezed through its first two games and appeared to be full of pregame energy. Down at the other end of the court, the Hudson City players were more subdued, going through their warm-up routine without a lot of yelling or even talking.

But that pregame demeanor was deceptive. Because it was Hudson City that came out roaring in the opening minutes and Camden that looked flat.

Fiorelli fired in a long three-pointer on the Hornets' first possession, and Jared cleanly blocked a shot on the other end. Spencer went end-to-end on a fast-break layup, then Ryan connected from the corner. It was 7–0 and barely a minute had gone by.

Camden called timeout. The spectators were quiet, stunned.

"Best team in the state," Spencer said firmly in the huddle.

"Us or them?" Fiorelli asked.

"Look at the scoreboard!" Spencer replied. "You tell me."

And Hudson City did look superior throughout the first half, extending the lead to eleven at one point before Camden began chipping away.

Dunk could feel the excitement growing as the second half unfolded. Camden was very good, no question about that, but Jared was having another big game inside and Fiorelli was on fire with seventeen points.

"We can win this thing," Dunk said to David, who was sitting next to him on the end of the bench.

David just nodded, his eyes never leaving the court. "Huge upset if we do," he said quietly. "*Huge.* Camden's a basketball factory."

"Changing of the guard, maybe."

"Yeah. But there's a long way to go. Six minutes."

"Six minutes?" said Dunk. "That's only about three minutes."

David rolled his eyes. "That joke's getting very old, Dunk." But he laughed anyway.

Dunk leaned forward on the bench, his hands clenched and his eyes intently watching the action on the court. Fiorelli was dribbling quickly across midcourt, head up, looking for an open man. Hudson City was ahead by four with just over a minute to play, but Camden was on an 8–3 run and had scrambled back into contention. The Camden fans were on their feet, shouting encouragement.

Fiorelli passed to Spencer in the corner, and Spencer dumped it in to Jared under the basket. Jared gave a quick head fake, and the Camden center bought it, leaving Jared an opening for an easy layup.

Dunk stood with the others and yelled. The game had tightened up in the second half, but a six-point lead in the final minute was huge.

Camden called timeout, and the Hudson City players ran to the bench and gathered around Coach Temple.

"Defense," he said. "This one's not over yet. Ryan, take a seat." Coach looked around. "Dunk, report in."

"Me?" Dunk asked, his eyes wide. Was he kidding?

"Go."

Dunk reported to the scorer's table and trotted back to the coach, who put his hand on Dunk's shoulder. "If they score, Fiorelli will in-bound the ball to you. Camden needs to foul or we'll just run out the clock. Protect the ball. Let them put you on the line."

Dunk swallowed hard and stepped onto the court. He looked at the clock: fifty-seven seconds. That seemed like an eternity. Dunk had been in awe of these players throughout the game. Now he was on the court with them, trying to preserve the biggest upset in the history of the tournament.

The other players were dripping with sweat, and their breathing was hot and furious. Dunk felt slower and more flat-footed than ever.

With a six-point lead, Hudson City expected the opponents to try for a quick three-pointer. So they were surprised when Camden's point guard passed the ball inside to the center, who banged home a layup despite Jared's furious defense.

"Be smart!" Spencer shouted as Fiorelli took the ball under the basket.

Dunk darted toward the end line. The Camden players were pressing, desperate to get the ball back, but Dunk was free and he took the pass and turned to dribble.

Two Camden players converged on him, stabbing at the ball and blocking his path. The ball was knocked loose, but an official blew his whistle, calling a foul.

Camden was over the foul limit. Dunk would be shooting two.

"Money in the bank," Spencer said, punching Dunk lightly on the shoulder.

"Automatic," said Fiorelli, jogging next to him toward the basket.

Dunk bit down on his lip and stepped to the line. His heart was pounding and his breathing was rapid, even though he'd only been in the game for a few seconds. His sweat felt cold. He had never expected to be in a situation like this.

He bounced the ball once, shut his eyes, and opened them. Checked his feet and eyed the rim. Tasted caramel corn and sausage.

The shot fell short, barely grazing the rim and falling to the floor. Worst shot he'd taken in months. The Hudson City fans groaned.

"No problem," said Willie. "Forget them jitters, Dunk."

The second shot was true, softly falling through the net and raising the lead to five points. The Hudson City players ran back on defense. Camden charged up the court.

The spectators were all standing now, pumping fists and screaming.

Willie and Spencer hounded the guards as they moved the ball around the perimeter, needing to shoot but cautious not to force one.

Dunk was near the basket, guarding a forward. The man darted out toward the free-throw line, then cut quickly back and headed toward the corner. Dunk tried to follow but ran squarely into the Camden center, who was setting a screen to free his teammate.

The pass went to the corner, and that forward was open. The three-pointer rolled around the rim and fell in. Dunk's fault. The lead was down to two.

What am I doing out here? Dunk wondered. *Nine great players and me.*

Sixteen seconds remained. Fiorelli faked a pass to Spencer, and Dunk's man took one step too many in that direction. So Dunk was open for the inbounds pass, and Fiorelli got him the ball. Again came the quick foul.

Dunk wiped his hands on his jersey and blinked. He felt like he'd swallowed some rocks.

Make two shots and this game was over. Miss one and Camden would still have a chance.

Dunk looked at the Hudson City bench, where his teammates were celebrating, high-fiving each other as their faces beamed, confident of the giant victory.

"All you!" shouted Coach Temple.

"Ninety-nine percent!" called Lamont.

Dunk's hands were shaking as he took the ball from the official. His armpits were dripping. This wasn't his driveway. It wasn't an empty court at the Y.

He knew the first shot was bad the instant it left his hands, drifting left and bonking off the side of the rim.

Dunk took a deep breath in an attempt to steady his nerves. Twenty-five thousand shots last year. Now all he needed was one.

The second shot looked good to him, arcing over the rim, right in the middle. It looked good to everybody in the gym.

But it wasn't. An inch too far, it hit solidly off the back of the rim and floated just beyond the front. Players leaped for the rebound and Jared got there first, tapping it hard.

In the scramble that followed, the Camden point guard came up with the ball, skipping past Spencer and Fiorelli and finding an open court ahead. The spectators were counting down the seconds—six, five, four—as Dunk and the others gave chase.

The guard had time for a game-tying layup and the path was clear, but he decided to take a chance. He stopped his dribble, faced the basket, and unleashed a perfect three-pointer that dropped cleanly through the net for the lead.

That was it. The horn sounded before Fiorelli could in-bound the ball. A six-point lead in the final minute had vanished completely. The

Hudson City players stood there stunned as the Camden players went wild.

Dunk felt like he could melt right there. They'd been counting on him—the free-throw specialist—and all he did was choke.

7
This Close

Dunk sat on the first row of the bleachers, staring at the floor and wishing he could just disappear instead of having to join his teammates for the somber ride back to the hotel.

Spencer had come over and poked his shoulder, mumbling, "Don't worry about it, man," but Dunk could hear the sadness in his voice.

Jared had said pretty much the same thing, taking a seat next to Dunk for a minute before heaving a sigh and walking toward the locker room.

And Coach Temple had even apologized. "I put you in a tough situation," he said. "You weren't ready; you were cold. I'm as much to blame as you are."

That hadn't made Dunk feel any better. Athletes are supposed to thrive on tough situations. He'd worked hard to be a guy that a coach and a team could count on. At least he thought he had.

So Dunk had no ambition to get off that bench. He was nearly in shock. The biggest upset possible had been right in their grasp, and he was the one who had squandered it.

"Are you stuck there?" came a cheery, familiar voice. Aunt Krystal was standing in front of him; he could tell by her red running shoes even though he didn't lift his head.

Dunk shook his head very slowly. "Hey," he whispered.

"Hey, yourself."

Now the tears came, filling his eyes and making his throat feel tight. He wiped at his eyes with his fists and sniffed. He glanced up at Krystal with a scowl that wasn't meant for her but was necessary to keep him from sobbing.

"I know how you feel," Krystal said. "Believe me."

Dunk looked back at the floor.

"I could drive you to the hotel if you want," she said.

Dunk shook his head again. "I'll take the bus with the team."

"I hoped you would."

"Did you find a room?"

"Yeah, at the Sea Breeze, a block away from where you're staying." She sat next to him and touched his shoulder.

"I let everybody down," he said.

Krystal didn't say anything to disagree. He glanced over at her and saw that she was thinking about how to respond. The worst thing she could have said was, "No you didn't" or "It's no big deal." He knew what he'd done. He knew how much it mattered.

So they both sat there quietly. Dunk felt miserable, but he was glad to see that Krystal could respect that feeling and not try to console him. She knew how much it mattered, too.

Dunk took the first full breath he'd allowed himself since the game ended. He looked up. Only a few people remained in the gym. Coach Temple was near the door talking to one of the Camden coaches. All of Dunk's teammates were outside.

"Guess we better go," Dunk said.

"Guess so. I'll see you at the hotel," Krystal said. "You guys going out for dinner or to the Boardwalk or what?"

"I got no appetite. I don't know what those guys are doing. I don't feel like doing *anything*."

"You have another game in the morning."

Dunk grimaced and let out his breath in a hurry. "That's just what I need," he said, meaning quite the opposite. "Maybe I can waste that opportunity, too."

* * *

Dunk was the last one on the bus, walking down the aisle past his teammates, who were spread out and dead-quiet, staring out the windows or at the seats in front of them.

Fiorelli stuck out his hand supportively for Dunk to smack, and Lamont slid over to make room next to him.

"Thanks," Dunk said, as much for not shunning him as for making room.

Lamont hadn't even played in the game, but he looked as glum as the starters. Stars or subs, they all wanted to win. They all had the same disappointment, knowing how close they'd come. They all would have shared that same triumph.

The bus pulled out of the YMCA parking lot.

Lamont put out his fist and Dunk met it with his. "No shame," Lamont said softly. "We came *this* close"—he held his thumb and first finger an eighth of an inch apart—"to beating the best team in the state."

"They knew we had 'em beat," Willie said

fiercely, kneeling on the seat in front of them and peering over. "You could see it on their faces. They thought they were going down."

Lamont and Dunk both nodded. Willie sat back down.

They all fell silent after that. It was the quietest bus ride these guys had ever been on.

The team went to Denny's for dinner. Dunk sat in a booth with Lamont and David and Miguel, but he barely picked at his hamburger and only ate a couple of fries.

After dinner, Willie and David left the room to join the others at the pool. They tried to talk Dunk into coming, but he begged off. "I'm tired," he said.

"You ain't tired," David replied. "Look, we all win or we all lose. Nobody's mad at you."

"*I'm* mad," Willie said. "Not at you, Dunk. Just that we lost. I felt like kicking out the windows on the bus I was so mad. But you ain't the enemy. Like David said, we ain't mad at *you*."

"Thanks," Dunk said. "Maybe I'll come out later. Let me be alone for a little while, you know?"

"Sure," Willie said. "I ain't gonna twist your arm or anything."

Dunk turned the TV to an old sitcom and lay back on the bed, barely paying attention to the show. He was hungry, but he still didn't want to eat.

After a few minutes there was a knock on the door. Dunk opened it to find Krystal waiting there.

"Your coach said I could take you for a walk," she said.

"I don't feel like walking."

"It'll do you some good to get out."

"Okay," he said. "Gotta find my sandals."

They walked up to the Boardwalk but didn't say much.

"Everybody okay?" Krystal asked.

"Yeah. Nobody blamed me."

"That's good."

"They *should* have," Dunk said. "They should be playing for the championship tomorrow, not in some worthless consolation game."

They sat on a Boardwalk bench, their backs to ocean, which was crashing a hundred yards behind them. Lots of people walked by—couples on vacation, groups of kids Dunk's age and younger, packs of teenagers, college kids. Everybody was having fun.

Except Dunk. He was still as down as could be.

"It cooled off," Krystal said. "Nice breeze coming in off the sea."

Dunk nodded and said, "Yeah," without any enthusiasm whatsoever.

Krystal turned to look at the water. The lights from the amusement pier illuminated some of the waves, and the red lights from a couple of boats could be seen way out near the horizon.

Four teenage boys were noisily playing touch football in the dark on the sand, knocking into one another and laughing.

"Big ocean," Krystal said.

Dunk looked, but then turned his gaze back to the boards beneath his feet. He folded his arms and held his chin in his hand.

"You remember a race I ran during my senior year in high school?" Krystal asked. "The county championships, remember?"

Dunk thought about it. "That time you lost?"

"That's the one. I got caught on the final straightaway of the four-hundred by that girl from Lincoln and I just folded up; finished *fourth!*"

"Yeah. Only race you lost the whole season, wasn't it?"

"Right. So you remember three weeks later in the sectionals, same situation, same girl? Remember what happened?"

"You smoked her," Dunk said.

"I did. I stewed about that collapse for three weeks, Cornell. I thought about it when I went to bed and dreamed about it all night. Woke up every morning in a sweat and carried that with me all day. And I ran with it in my head during every workout, fought twice as hard as I ever did to make sure it would never happen again."

Dunk nodded slowly. He wiped a tear from his eye with his thumb. "You're lucky you had a chance to make up for it," he said. "This one's gonna haunt me for a long, long time."

"It'll go faster than you think," Krystal said. "It hurts like crazy right now, but I'm telling you the truth. That hurt is what's going to make you a better basketball player than you'd ever be without it. It's going to drive you, Cornell. I can see it."

He stared across the Boardwalk at a stand where players were lined up to shoot water guns at targets that would propel small mechanical horses toward a finish line. The barker was calling to people in the crowd, trying to get two more players for the race. Sixties rock music was blaring from the speakers.

"You're right," Dunk said. "When that game ended I thought I'd never want to play basketball again. Forget it ever happened. Now I can't wait to get back to it. Get a chance to redeem myself."

"Tomorrow morning," Krystal said.

"Nah," Dunk replied. "I probably won't even play in that game. What I mean is, the next season is a long way off. I'm going to have to live with this for a while."

"Live with it, yeah. Kick it in the butt every time you get on the court. You don't *want* to forget what happened. You want it hanging there to remind you how hard you have to work to get past it."

Dunk's eyes opened a little wider. He bit down on his lip. "I hear you."

"How'd you even make this team in the first

place, Cornell? As I remember you were the worst of the worst a year ago."

Dunk gave a slight smile. "Was I that bad?"

"You weren't good. Took about a thousand hours of practice just to learn to shoot free throws, didn't it?"

Dunk's smile got wider. "I think I learned a little faster than that."

"Still can't jump," Krystal said. "Still can't run. Got a long way to go, I'd say."

"Whoa," Dunk said, leaning back in mock surprise. "Getting tough on me, aren't you?"

Krystal put her arm around him. "Maybe you're finally getting tough enough to take it, nephew. See, there's more to life than free throws. There's more to *basketball* than free throws. That's a good place to start, though. Now we just move on from here."

8

Back on the Horse

Coach Temple had a surprise for the team as they gathered in the locker room before the consolation game.

"Miguel and David will be the starting guards," he said. "This is not a demotion for Willie or Spencer or anybody else. But we've all worked hard and we all deserve some quality playing time, especially since the title is out of our reach."

Spencer looked surprised, but he didn't balk. Willie put up his hand.

"Yes, Willie?"

"Will we play at all?"

"Sure. Everybody will play a lot today. But I'm not done naming the starters yet."

"You're benching us, too?" Fiorelli asked.

"Not benching. Just spreading things out. We're going with Lamont and Dunk at forward. Louie at center."

Dunk's eyes got wide and he felt a tightening in his gut, but that quickly went away. Jared gave him a light jab with his elbow and said, "It's all you, bro."

"You got it," Dunk replied.

"We're not conceding anything," Coach said. "Third is better than fourth. But last night was wrenching. Let's take the pressure off and *enjoy* this game. I don't expect any falloff just because we're starting five new guys. Everybody on this team is good."

Dunk stood and walked with the others to the gym. He was excited but scared. This was unexpected.

Montclair had won its first two games but had fallen to Burlington in the semifinal. So the two North Jersey teams would be playing for third place in the tournament.

And though he knew it was just a consolation game, meaningless to anyone but those involved, Dunk couldn't help but feel as energized as if he were competing for a state title. What a difference to know in advance that he'd be playing an important role. Not like last night when he'd been caught off guard and unready at a crucial moment.

"Thanks, Coach," he said, falling in step with Coach Temple as they entered the gym.

"Right back on the horse," Coach said. "Put last night behind you."

"That's where it is, but I won't ever forget it. I'm ready."

Dunk stood near the basket and rebounded for his teammates, who were firing up jump shots. The bleachers were nearly empty. Most of the Hudson City fans had gone home after last night's game, and the bigger crowd for the championship game hadn't arrived yet. Aunt Krystal was seated behind the Hornets' bench.

"Guess it's up to us," said Louie Gonzalez, joining Dunk under the basket. Louie had not played since the opening game against Salem, and even then he'd only been on the court for a couple of minutes.

"We'll be fine," Dunk said. "Usually the nervousness goes away once the game starts."

"Hope so," said Louie. He wiped his hand across the top of his big round head. Like Dunk, he was tall but chunky, not very quick or limber. His feet were huge for a twelve-year-old. "I'm so nervous I could puke."

Dunk smiled. "Aim for a Montclair guy if you do."

Louie swallowed and nodded. "I'll be all right," he said. "Maybe Montclair will start their subs, too."

But that was not the case. Montclair sent its

regular lineup onto the floor. Dunk looked at the opposing five as they lined up for the jump ball. They looked very competitive and athletic.

The guy lined up next to Dunk was about his height, but his shoulders were higher and his stomach was taut. Even his fingers looked more athletic—longer and stronger, as if he could grip that basketball like a vise or yank it out of your hands.

Now the ball was coming their way, tapped easily away from Louie by the Montclair center. Dunk's man grabbed it and pivoted quickly, darting toward the basket as Dunk stumbled and then gave chase.

Lamont ran over to stop the rush to the hoop, leaving his own man uncovered.

"Switch!" Lamont called, and Dunk ran over to pick up the other forward.

David had already tried to make the same switch. The chaos left a guard wide open near the foul line, and that's where the ball went. But he missed the open shot and Louie grabbed the rebound, hugging the ball to his chest and looking for someone to pass to.

Miguel took the ball and gave Louie a relieved grin. "Survived that one," he said. Of today's starters, Miguel had the most experience, having been the first sub off the bench in the first three games and playing significant minutes. He dribbled across the midcourt line and passed the ball to David.

Dunk fought for position near the basket, but Montclair's man-to-man defense was tough. Sneakers squeaked on the wood floor and elbows flew.

"Let's see some motion!" Miguel called. He had the ball again and was dribbling at the top of the key, eager to pass the ball inside. But nobody was close to being open.

Lamont drifted outside and the ball went to him. His shot was off target, smacking the side of the rim.

The Montclair center ripped down the rebound and made the quick outlet pass to the point guard, who led a fast break. But an errant pass went right into David's hands, and the momentum swung back the other way.

Dunk hadn't even reached midcourt yet, but this time his slowness was to Hudson City's advantage. While the rest of the players were racing up the court, he and Louie had been caught flat-footed. So they were both wide open, and David's pass found Dunk, who took three dribbles and made an easy layup.

He slapped hands with Louie and ran back on defense as fast as he could.

The Montclair coach was standing in front of the bench and yelling at his players. "You're out of control," he said. "Settle down."

The point guard nodded as he dribbled past. He called out a play number and made a sharp pass to the corner.

Montclair clearly had the better talent on the

floor, but their shooting remained cold. By the midpoint of the first quarter their lead was only 7–4.

Ryan, Jared, and Spencer reported in at the next stoppage, sending Dunk to the bench along with David and Louie.

"Nice job," Coach Temple said as they took seats on the bench. "Stay ready, men. You aren't done yet."

Dunk grabbed a water bottle and sucked half of it down, then wiped his face with a towel. He raised a fist and brought it down on top of Louie's, then did the same to David. They'd played well. No embarrassment this time. This game wasn't meaningless. Not to them.

Then he felt a hand on his shoulder. "You got promoted, huh?" asked Krystal.

"Nah," Dunk said. "I know where I stand." He pointed to the court, where Jared was racing past with the ball. "These guys are good. Give me another thousand hours or two. Then we'll see where I'm at."

"Looking good so far," Krystal said. "Keep at it."

Coach Temple substituted freely throughout the first half, and Dunk got a couple of more minutes late in the second quarter. Montclair did not let up at all, however, and built a ten-point lead by halftime.

Dunk held his head high as they left the court for the locker room. But his gaze fell on the basket at the far end of the court. The basket where he'd missed those crucial free throws the night before. Hudson City would be shooting at that basket in the second half. He might just find himself at that line again.

"We're looking like a team," Coach said in the locker room. "We'll see if we can make a run at them in the second half, but I'm still planning to use everybody. We'll go with our usual starting lineup at the beginning, but all twelve men will play. Keep digging and scrapping. Keep chasing after those loose balls."

Jared came alive in the third quarter and

dominated the inside. His thundering rebounds and a driving put-back worked the deficit down to four points.

"Dunk and Miguel," Coach called. "Give Ryan and Spencer a breather. Report in."

They crouched by the scorer's table, waiting for a timeout or a foul. The third quarter was nearly over when they finally went in. Fiorelli's jumper had brought Hudson City to within two.

The Montclair players looked frustrated, having let a comfortable lead slip away. And Jared was as competitive as always, so the play under the boards was physical. Dunk got shoved but he shoved right back. The ball was in the air. Jared brought it down.

"Smart now!" Miguel said as he took Jared's pass and moved up the court.

"Fourteen seconds!" yelled Coach Temple. "Plenty of time. Good shot."

Fiorelli set a screen and Jared fought past it, finding a brief opening and taking Miguel's bounce pass. He pivoted and shot, but the ball hit the backboard hard and deflected off the rim.

Jared's move had brought Montclair's big men to the right side of the hoop, but the ball came down to the left. Dunk grabbed it. Time was running out.

Dunk was in the paint with the ball, trying to out-muscle the man who was guarding him. It was like pushing against a wall, but Dunk gave a juke to his left and then swung right, finding enough freedom to get off a shot with a hand in his face and another in his rib cage.

The shot missed, bonking off the backboard and falling to the floor. But Dunk had been fouled. The referee's whistle halted the action with three seconds left in the quarter.

Dunk stepped to the line. The buzzer sounded and Lamont ran onto the court. He pointed toward Fiorelli, who had his hands on his knees and was puffing. Fiorelli blinked his eyes quickly and walked off the floor.

Dunk stared at the basket, the one where he'd missed those three shots last night. He took a deep breath and let it out. His heart was beating hard, as much from anxiety as the running.

He made the first shot and looked quickly toward the ceiling with relief, shaking his wrists and feeling a nice surge of adrenaline.

"Yes, Dunk!" came a cry from the bench.

"Back at it!" said Lamont, who was lined up to Dunk's right.

Dunk calmly made the second shot. He turned and watched for his man, but the horn sounded to end the quarter before Montclair could get off a shot.

Dunk looked at the scoreboard. The game was tied. What a difference.

Last night seemed like a million years ago.

Coach Temple's strategy was paying off. While the Montclair starters were worn down playing their fourth hard game in three days, the

Hudson City subs were fresher and very eager to prove themselves. Lamont in particular was having a big game—nine points and six rebounds.

And when David hit a three-pointer late in the fourth quarter, the Hornets had their largest lead of the game, 49–44. Willie and Jared were the only regular starters on the floor.

"Dunk, go in for Louie," Coach said.

Dunk popped up and waited by the scorer's table. The bleachers were filling up now; fans from Camden and Burlington waiting for the title game that would follow.

Third place is better than fourth. Dunk recalled Coach Temple's words. Coach had taken a chance today, letting his backup players do so much of the work. Dunk wasn't about to let that be a bad decision. He'd do everything he could to help preserve this win.

Montclair's point guard was at the line when Dunk took the floor. Less than a minute remained. He hugged Louie as he sent him to the bench, and Louie patted his shoulder.

"We pulled this off," Dunk said. "We're gonna win this one."

The first free throw was good, but the second bounced high off the rim. Dunk boxed out the man beside him and leaped for it, getting up higher than he ever had in his life. He hauled the ball down with his right hand and brought it to his chest, elbows up, protecting his prize.

Willie raced over behind Dunk and hollered for the ball. The players on the Hudson City bench stood and clapped, knowing that this one was as good as over. The lead was four. Montclair was out of gas. Hudson City had the ball and the momentum.

Time was running out. Willie, Lamont, and Miguel worked the ball around the perimeter, killing precious seconds. Montclair had to foul.

The ball came to Dunk. No reason to shoot, so he dribbled toward the corner. The Montclair bench was yelling for their players to foul to stop the clock. Finally someone grabbed Dunk's arm.

The whistle blew. Dunk tossed the ball to the referee and walked to the line.

"Ninety-nine percent!" yelled Lamont.

"Like a robot!" called Fiorelli.

Dunk smiled and glanced at the clock. Eight more seconds. Willie smacked him on the shoulder. Jared made a fist and shook it.

Both shots were identical. Nothing but net. After the second one swished, the buzzer sounded. Louie came back into the game, pointing to Dunk and grinning.

The Hudson City players gave Dunk a standing ovation as he walked off the floor.

He hugged his coach and sat down.

9
Credentials

*T*hey had checked out of the hotel before the game, but Coach Temple had promised three hours to enjoy the beach and Boardwalk before making the trip back to Hudson City. Each Hornet player had been presented with a third-place medal right after Camden wrapped up the title over Burlington.

"That could have been us," Fiorelli said, watching the Camden coach and players accept the championship trophy.

"We know that," Spencer said. "We were at

least the second-best team in this tournament. Next time we win it, right?"

"You got it." Fiorelli had his bronze medal around his neck, hanging from its red-and-white ribbon.

"Don't go wearing that thing in the ocean," Dunk said. "One hard wave and it's lost."

Dunk wasn't thinking about the beach yet, though. His stomach was rumbling with hunger. He'd eaten very little since yesterday afternoon.

He walked out of the YMCA with Krystal. "You're not going straight home, are you?" he asked her.

"I guess not," she said. "I'll at least eat with you before driving back."

"So meet us at the Boardwalk. By that big food stand next to the arcade."

The mood on the bus was very different this time. The Hudson City players were back to their usual selves, loose and joking and relaxed.

"That was, like, an *intense* couple of days,"

Fiorelli was saying. "I mean, it's tough enough trying to win games against teams you see two or three times a season. Then you get down here and you don't know what to expect. Every time we took the floor I was shaking. I was like, 'We could get clobbered here. These guys look awesome.'"

"That tells you something, don't it?" Willie said. "Because we played everybody tough. We got what it takes. We can think beyond our own neighborhood now. We got *credentials*."

That got Dunk to thinking about his own "credentials." He'd played a good game this morning, but he knew that he had a long way to go before reaching the level that Jared and Fiorelli and Spencer were on. Those guys could hold their own with the best players in the state. Dunk was still pretty average.

He knew what he needed to work on:

—Speed. That was one thing he could certainly improve. It was a matter of getting into better condition. Running after school. Keeping up the hustle on the court.

—Flexibility. Especially his jumping ability. This was still his weakest aspect. But he knew where he could work on it. The guys would never let him hear the end of it if they caught him, but Aunt Krystal's aerobics classes would definitely limber him up.

He laughed at that, picturing himself dancing and bounding and bouncing around the gym to the salsa and rock tunes Krystal played. But if it would make him a better athlete, he'd be willing to give it a try.

—Basketball. As long as he kept playing, he'd keep getting better. There was always a pickup game to jump into outside the Y or at a playground. He'd never get tired of that.

"Who's playing tomorrow?" Dunk said loudly. "Ten o'clock at the Y. Who's up for it?"

"Not me," said Fiorelli. "I got blisters on the bottoms of my feet. And football practice starts in a couple of days. I need a break."

"I'll be there," said Willie.

"Me, too," said Lamont.

"Now shut up about basketball," David called. "It's summertime. Time to chill out on the beach."

Dunk met Krystal at the food stand while the others ran toward the water. He'd join them later.

"My turn to buy?" Dunk asked. "You got the Chinese food the other night."

"I can handle it," Krystal said. "You must be just about tapped out anyway."

Dunk's parents had given him forty dollars for food and he still had a few bucks left. He shrugged. "I'll get it next time then. There's a few cars I can wash this weekend to make some money."

"You can wash mine."

"Bring it over."

They drank big cups of icy lemonade and shared a plate of fried clams and onion rings. Then Dunk had a sausage sandwich.

"Lot of grease," he said, wiping his mouth with a napkin.

"Tell me about it," Krystal said, patting her narrow stomach. "That was my one indulgence for the summer."

Krystal paid the bill and said she'd better get going.

"One more thing," Dunk said.

"You're not full yet?"

"Not food," he said. "Follow me."

They walked a short way up the Boardwalk and stopped at the basketball shoot. Dunk paid a dollar and said, "Watch this."

His first shot had the nice, true arc. It bounced lightly on the back of the rim, rolled slightly to the left, then dropped through the net.

"Nice touch," Krystal said.

Dunk took the second ball, crouched slightly, and flicked his wrist with confidence. This one fell cleanly through.

"We have a winner!" shouted the guy in charge. "Take anything in the booth!"

Dunk turned to Krystal and grinned. "Whatever you want," he said.

She laughed. There were purple gorillas, a green moose in a Knicks jersey, and dozens of big teddy bears and tigers.

"That moose looks a little like you," she teased. "I guess I'll take that one."

Dunk grabbed the moose and handed it to her. "Thanks, Aunt Krystal," he said.

"What are you thanking me for?" she asked. "You're the one giving me a gift."

"You know why," Dunk said.

She gave a sly smile. "The lemonade?"

Dunk rolled his eyes. "Give me that moose," he said. "I'll carry it to your car for you. And really—thanks for everything. For believing in me. It means a lot coming from you."

They walked back to the Sea Breeze Motel. The car was boiling hot from sitting in the sun, so Krystal opened the windows and turned on the air conditioner, then stepped outside and gave Dunk a hug.

"Drive carefully," he said.

"Have a great afternoon. Put on your lotion."

"I already did." Dunk set the moose on the passenger seat and clicked on its seat belt. "He'll keep you company," he said.

And as he walked back toward the beach, Dunk felt taller somehow. More of a man than when they'd left Hudson City, just a few days before. He could hear the music from the Boardwalk and smell the salt air of the ocean, and the sun on his shoulders was hot and penetrating.

Cars were parked in every available space on these side streets. The beach would be packed with vacationers. Among them were a dozen

Hudson City basketball players and their coaches.

Dunk walked faster now. He couldn't wait to rejoin his teammates. A couple of hours of splashing in the waves. Joking, hollering, feeling the wet sand between their toes. Maybe an ice-cream cone or a milk shake. More sunburn.

Then back to the bus, in their damp shorts and with sand in their shoes. Back up the Parkway. Back to familiar ground.

Back home to Hudson City.

* * *

Read an excerpt from

TAKEDOWN

Winning Season #8

Could anything be harder than this?

Donald sat with his back against the gymnasium wall, eyes shut and sweat streaming down his face. His legs hurt. His shoulders ached. His left foot was starting to cramp.

He opened one eye and looked at the clock on the wall: 4:27 P.M. Coach Mills had said practice would end at five. Three minutes of rest and then thirty more minutes of conditioning drills.

There was an inch of water left in his bottle, and he sucked it right down. The water was warm but it quenched his thirst a little. The corner of his mouth stung where the bottle had touched it. He put a finger to his lip. When he pulled it away there was a dot of red. He curled his tongue to that spot and tasted blood.

I'll live, he thought.

He felt a shoe against his leg—not quite a kick, but a rather hard nudge. Freddy Salinardi was standing there, peering down at him. Freddy was an eighth-grader and one of the team captains. "Let's go, wimp," he said. "Nap time is over."

Donald scrambled to his feet. Freddy called everybody wimps, at least all of the seventh-graders. This was the first day of practice, so the newcomers were getting tested by the veterans. Donald stepped toward the mat. Freddy was already hassling Mario and Kendrick, making them stand up, too.

What a jerk, Donald thought, but he'd never say that out loud.

He had already started to figure things out. Coach worked the wrestlers hard but he was a nice guy, and he certainly seemed to know his stuff about the sport. But he let the eighth-graders push the younger guys around. That seemed to be how he kept order.

They'd learned some basic wrestling moves earlier in the session, but the past half hour had been all about conditioning. Jumping jacks, sit-ups, running in place. Donald knew this sport would be difficult, but he hadn't envisioned anything like this.

"Line up!" Coach called. "The fun starts now."

Donald joined the others in a straight line against the wall.

"What now?" asked Mario, tugging on Donald's arm.

Donald turned and shrugged. Mario was one the few kids here who was shorter than Donald, but he was stockier. His dark curly hair was matted to his forehead with sweat.

"Some new form of torture," Donald whispered.

Coach was looking over the thirty or so wrestlers, sizing them up with a smug smile. He was young—three years earlier he'd still been wrestling for the college team at Montclair State—and had the build of a solid 140-pounder. "Nobody said this would be easy, right? You new guys are getting a taste of how tough this sport is. You can't even begin to be a good wrestler until you get into shape. The whole key is conditioning. Without that, you're nothing."

Coach pointed to Kendrick, a quiet newcomer to Hudson City who sat next to Donald in English class. "What's your favorite sport?" he asked.

Kendrick looked around and scrunched up his mouth before answering. "Wrestling?"

"Is that a question or a statement?"

"A statement, I guess."

"Good answer."

Now Coach looked at Donald. "What's your least favorite sport?"

Donald put a finger to his chest as he asked weakly, "Me?"

"Yeah, you."

At this point Donald could have said wrestling and he wouldn't have been lying. But he said "track," which would have been true any other time. His best friend Manny Ramos was a standout distance runner, but Donald had wanted no part of that sport, despite Manny's frequent urging to join him at it.

Coach's smile got broader. "That's too bad," he said, "because guess what? Wrestlers run their butts off."

Coach made a circular motion with his hand. "Laps around the gym," he said. "A nice steady pace. We're not racing here, just staying in motion."

There was a collective groan from the group, but all of them started jogging. The gym was small and the corners were tight, but the jogging did seem easier to Donald than all those calisthenics.

That changed in a hurry when Coach gave his next directive. "Every time I blow my whistle, I want you all to drop and give me five push-ups.

Then pop up and get right back to the running. Start now." And he blew his whistle.

Donald dropped with the others and managed the five push-ups, feeling the strain all the way from his shoulders down to his fingers.

Why am I doing this? he wondered.

He kept wondering that for fifteen more minutes as they alternated running with push-ups. But when the session finally ended and he looked around at the exhausted wrestlers making their way to the locker room, he couldn't help but feel more than a little bit proud to be one of them.

* * *

RICH WALLACE was a high school and college athlete and then a sportswriter before he began writing novels. He is the author of many critically acclaimed sports-themed novels, including *Wrestling Sturbridge, Shots on Goal,* and *Restless: A Ghost's Story.* Wallace lives with his family in Honesdale, Pennsylvania.